Christina Snitko

MIRAGES

Bagriy & Company
Chicago
2021

MIRAGES
by Christina Snitko

Copyright © 2021 by Christina Snitko

ISBN 978-1-7366974-0-5

Book & Cover Design by Yulia Tymoshenko © 2021

Drawings by Kasey Williams © 2021

Published by
Bagriy & Company
Chicago, Illinois
www.bagriycompany.com

Printed in the United States of America

Table of Contents

The Mask You Wore 11

Illusions of the Sun 89

The Balance of Existence 147

New Beginnings 189

This book is dedicated to all of the souls who know what it is like to experience a darkness so vast, that it seems absolutely infinite. Although darkness likes to tell you otherwise, please know that you are not alone. You are never alone. I am saying this, not to diminish your own experiences, but instead, to validate them. I hope that through reading my words, you too can realize this. But I also hope you can become empowered enough to uncover the innate power, worth and truth that you all carry. You are so powerful. Please do not ever forget that.

All of my love,
Christina Snitko

Here I am
Standing naked in front of you
With nothing but my words
Wrapped around my truth

~Vulnerability

THE MASK
YOU WORE

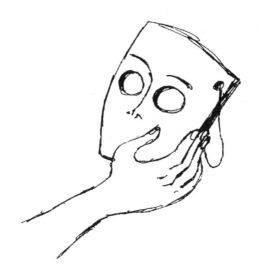

I thought I knew what happiness was like
The first time around
I could feel it and remember it so vividly
I was sure that it couldn't possibly be anything else
But later I came to realize
That it wasn't happiness
It was just blindly falling
Before I hit the ground.

~ *The falling before the landing.*

I remember how badly
I wanted you
  To dance with me

  But you refused.

  Not the first time
  You had
  Disappointed me

  ~*Coney Island*

You had so much potential
What was so disappointing
Was you not seeing it
But then I realized
You never really wanted to

~It truly is a shame how much potential can go to waste.

We had a wonderful future
Planned together
But you cared more about your own
Than the one
We could have built together

The sad reality of life
Is that you can give all of yourself
To a person
That you thought you knew

The tragedy here
Is not giving all of yourself
To that particular person
No

The tragedy is
Finding out
That particular person
That you thought you had known

Was never that person
That you fell for
At all

My skin was too soft
For your rough hands to touch.

~*You should have never crossed my boundaries.*

You loved my body.
I could see that
But what I truly wanted,
Was for you
To love my soul.

You fell in love with my light
I had so much of it
That I was glowing
At first, I thought you fell for my soul
But little did I know
You had a plan
I was just oblivious to see it
You were fascinated by my light
Curious even
How could someone
Have so much of it?
Because in a world full of darkness
There is no way one could have so much light
You had never seen that before
And that is why you chose me
To lighten up the darkness inside your soul
I should have fucking known
That you were a thief
You were devious
Slowly stealing some of the light that I shone
Like a child stealing pennies
Little by little
You needed my light

To escape your darkness
Because you couldn't even face it, yourself
You had none of your own
So, you took mine
Until I had nothing left
You started the destruction, of myself
And I fell down into the black hole
With no escape out.

~You were the black hole that sucked my light out.

I remember when I first noticed that your eyes were different. The room was dim and not much could be seen. Except for your eyes. Your pupils were so big, that your eyes looked like an endless sea of darkness. There was no room left for anything else. Just the darkness. I looked into your eyes more carefully, wondering if I could see my reflection in them. But I found nothing. All I could see was the darkness. Your eyes were the black holes that sucked out all of the energy that I ever had. And when the light came on, it exposed my shame. Like a spotlight for all of the wrong that I had done. They say your body is a temple, and I let you in. But little did I know, that the more I let you in, those dark eyes consumed more and more of my light. You were always starving, ravenous for more. The more that I gave you, the more I started to turn cold. Darkness then started to creep in, because darkness likes the cold. Darkness continued to be with me, until I realized that it would be my guest for a long time.

I denied that I lived in darkness, because we are taught that darkness is inferior to light. Light is where we need to reach to. But reaching too high for that light can get you burned too.

I wanted to reach for that light. I hated the darkness that I had created. I clung to the light, as if it was my only hope for life. But even then too, it slipped away from my fingers.

I then realized that maybe darkness wasn't so bad. Maybe that is what I deserved, since even the light didn't want to stay with me. I pushed everything good away, because I felt like I wasn't worthy for the good anymore. Darkness was where I needed to stay.

Darkness was my temporary home. But at that point in time, nothing felt more permanent than that. *I'll take care of you* it whispered, as it hugged my soul. So, I let the darkness control me and consume me, until it was completely me. I was the darkness. Nothing else could pass through. And that's when I realized, that's what it was like, when I was with you.

~My time in the black hole of the universe.

You would make a great actor
For all of the lies you told me
I believed them
Full heartedly
You were good at playing
A character of your choice
For I thought it was you
All along
But even the greatest actors
Can't keep their face up
For too long

~ The mask you wore.

I should have realized
That there was something wrong
When I felt lonelier with you
Than I already did
On my own

How long will I have to
Wait for you?
Or will the universe
Test me once more
Just when I think
I have gotten it all
Figured out
You, the figure of deceit
Like to play
These games with me
Making me think
That I finally found
My happiness
And then
Take it away
From me

~Somewhere in between

How many times will you break my heart?
Telling me you are a man
    That is worth my time
    But honey
    With every action
    And every lie
    You prove to me
    More and more
    That you will never
    Be mine

I caused my own heartbreak, by believing you would save me.

You set me on fire and then blamed me for being careless with the matches.

~*Gaslighting*

You liked to play with me
For I was a marionette
On your puppet string
You
Controlling my every move
Making me believe
That it was I
Making your decisions
You had your experience
And had your fun
But I cut off my strings
From your pathetic little show
I was done being a doll
That you thought you could
Play with

~*Puppet Act*

I was a rose
Beautiful but harsh
Admired but cold
From far away
People could only notice
The elegance
The shape
The look of who I was
And they liked it
You did too
As you showed me off
Claimed your prize to the world
Marked me
To show
That you owned me
Because deep down inside
You knew
You never deserved me
You turned the everlasting rose
Into one that was sure to die
I wilted
But my thorns remained

~You used me.

It's too fucking late
For you to come back
And say that you have changed

We had a timeline
And yours has expired
So leave, and never come back

Take all of your fucking lies
And whatever else
You have conspired

~I am done.

You don't see the tears behind the porcelain doll's eyes. She looks perfect on the exterior, so you think there is nothing wrong with her. You don't see the cracks that live between her heart and soul. You don't realize, how on most days, the smile that is painted on her face, is fake. This doll is smiling, because it is the only thing that is keeping her from falling apart. From shattering into thousands of pieces of porcelain. Pieces, that will never be able to come back together again.

~ The insane amount of effort it takes, to hold yourself together.

I'd like to think
That if it was fate
Time will bring us back
Together again

But how long do I
Keep holding on?
Until it is time
To fully let go?

I am tired of waiting
Praying
That our universes
Will collide again

I am beginning to lose faith
As the light years grow bigger
And bigger between us
Until there is nothing left

And pretty soon I realize
That the space between us
Will continuously grow
So big

And so far
That our paths
Will never cross
Together again

Maybe I had rose colored glasses
As I missed all the flags
Maybe I was a hopeless romantic
And went a little mad

I am trying to remember
What even was it
That made me fall for you?
My chest starts to tighten
I don't know what to do

Were you always like this?
Or did the honeymoon phase wear off?
Because if that was true babe
That means it was never love.

~I was blind.

The wolf devoured my flesh
And left me with nothing

~*Only bones were left behind.*

Your face still haunts me
Within my pleasant dreams
I wish I could forget
All of the wrong
You had done to me
For you held your pride
On this pedestal
I could not touch
But what you had wanted
Was to have power
That was stimulated
By your lust
What I realized was
Not only were you not
Even capable of love
You were not fully capable
To even fucking trust

~Mad King

I was an oasis
For your thirsty soul
You needed to drink me
So that you could feel whole

But if you abuse an oasis
It will eventually run dry
And soon there was nothing
Left for me to cry

~Numb

You used your words like honey
To trap me by your sweetness
You are nothing but a liar
Being alone was your weakness

You should have known
That I was too bright for your soul
Your love was an illusion
You needed me to feel whole

You were like a vampire
Feasting on my blood
Your heart was too cold
To even know how to love

Although I now stand
With two feet on the ground
I am still lost
Waiting to be found

I was a lush forest
But now I am a desert
What used to be me
Is no longer present

~ The life force that was sucked out of me.

Your biggest mistake, was not realizing that you had the whole entire galaxy in your hands, because you were too busy chasing the stars.

~You cannot get back what you had freely lost.

I hope her stars shine brighter for you
Since mine never did.

~You took me for granted. I hope she satisfies you.

You will remember me
Yes
Because
You will be haunted
By
Me

I have mastered the art of crying, without making a sound.

~Not wanting to be a burden.

I went outside and listened to music
Until I was chilled to the bone
 At least I was able to feel the cold
 When I couldn't feel
 Anything else
 At all

 ~At least it was something.

Please give me the antidote to my pain.

She used to take her coffee sweet
When her soul still had
   Innocence and youth
   She used to love the taste
   As the sugar reminded her
   Of being a kid

   But as life goes on
   And hearts get broken
   As you get lost
   You then start to harden

   The sweet coffee you once loved
   No longer tastes like youth
   And you need something stronger
   To get you through your days

   The coffee you once tasted
   That reminded you of hazelnuts
   Of your short childhood
   That people made fun of

Is no longer the color
Of a birch tree
It is now the color
Of a dark oak

~Evolution into adulthood.

She tries to numb her pain
With a bottle of alcohol
She wondered if her life
Was even worth living at all?

How are some so lucky?
While others are plain fools?
It is all too much
To be playing by the rules

She was so full of life
But the world had feasted
On her precious soul

She could not even remember
What it was like
To feel fully whole

There are no genies to grant wishes
Her innocence long gone
She just wanted to go back
To when she was young

She lives in her melancholy
Since no one understands
What it's like to be her
As her universe expands

She had a good heart
She was a hopeless romantic
She was one of a kind
She believed in the magic

She was the rare one
Who never came to play
But life kept on failing her
Soon, her color turned gray

It was only a matter of time
Before her cup became empty
There was nothing left to say
But her eyes spoke plenty

Her spark now gone
She no longer wants to fight
She is exhausted
And wants to say *Goodnight*

I'm trying to understand
The labyrinth called my mind
But I am lost within the maze
Like a puzzle piece you cannot find

I used to be quite influenced
By the lies you told to me
But there is nothing left now
Of what I used to be

If only there was a way
I could turn off all the lights
So I can sit within the darkness
And say hello to the night

I am tired of fighting
This war has to end
I am suffocating trying
I'm just playing pretend

I used to before
Find people to fix
But now I need someone
Because I'm losing my grip

I used to be full of light
Now there is nothing but darkness
I have nothing left to give
A beautiful soul now haunted

That's the thing about people
That hurt you so bad
While you are left bleeding
They walk away unscathed

Is anybody out there?
Who won't cause me pain?
There were people of my past
That have poisoned my brain

This is my cry for help
I just ask of one thing
Don't let me drown tonight
Help me stay sane

I gave you the seeds to plant
The flowers of happiness in your heart
But you are the one that chose
To throw away these seeds
And live within your sadness
My soul is filled with gardens
So fucking beautiful
It is a wonderland
One cannot describe
But this wonderland
Is enchanted
Not everyone
Can enter
But I let you in
And you started to wilt all of my flowers
Just with your touch
My wonderland has no room
For the coldness that resides
Within your heart
I had to banish your coldness
Before any more of my flowers
Would die
I do not miss you

I just miss the potential
Of what could have been
But darling
May everyone know
That falling in love with potential
Is a dangerous thing
Because you fall in love
With what is not there
Which ultimately resides
In you
Breaking
Your own heart

We were too busy
Being infatuated with one another
That when we built our foundation
It wasn't strong enough
And eventually
As that infatuation wore off
Our foundation started to crumble
Under that tension
That we both seemed to hold
Then the fights started to come out
From the issues and burdens we chose to carry
We both carried our pride
When we should have carried each other
Then soon
There was nothing left
To hold our relationship together
Like a house of cards
All that we had
Fell completely apart
When you are standing
Within this brokenness
You have two choices:
To either fix what has been broken

Or just leave
Some things that are broken
Are no longer
Meant to be together
Our pieces were too shattered
They caused cuts in my hand
As I really did try
To put them back together
And that was when I realized
That it was better
For me to just leave
As this was no longer
Our story
Anymore

I was lost in a minute
In your ocean blue eyes
 Was thinking about a future
 Wanted something to call mine

The universe likes to play
These cruel games with us
Pulling us apart
When love wasn't enough

And maybe it wasn't fate
Just an illusion of what could be
Maybe you were bored
And never really loved me

I'm not a figurine
In your complicated game
I'm a person with feelings
That one needs to tame

When will men learn
To stop fucking with our feelings?
My heart has no strength
To be constantly healing

Healing from the lies
And healing from the pain
Soon there will be nothing
Left of my remains

You suffer in silence
And paint on your fake smile
You are a fool for believing
That a boy is worthwhile

It's like a game of chess
Only you don't know how to play
You're supposed to guard your queen
But you threw her away

Like a luxury brand item
You started off high
But then you lowered your price
And in came the lies

Being an empath is hard
You just feel it all too much
In this modern world
The game is too rough

You are out of all your moves
Now stuck in a stalemate
You know you're going to lose
But you aren't ready for your fate

You're tired of this game
And you no longer want to play
You wonder if there is a reason
For you to even stay

As fast as a flame can ignite
It can expire just as soon
And while we were happy at one point
I will never go back to June

We were drunk on our love
Planned our future together
We were taking on the world
We were ready for forever

You started to tear down my walls
And mend the cracks of my heart
And when I was just about ready
You tore me apart

You used me as a distraction
Until she had returned
And all that was left
Were the remains that you burned

You threw away my love
Made me think you were my savior
Maybe it was fun for you
But you will regret all this later

I'm sorry I wasn't enough for you
And that she had won
But I will not be waiting for you
When you realize that I was the one

Erase me out of your memory
Remove me from your pain
    Our worlds may have collided
    But heartbreak remains

    Please forget me
    And what I was to you
    You deserve to be happy
    Now that we are through

    And maybe one day
    We might meet again
    As different life forms
    Or as the wind blows

    You will then see me
    Transparent as a ghost

    And hopefully you will realize
    That you never truly had me
    I was really only
    What you had wanted to see

Nothing but a mirage
I was there
And then I was gone.

You weren't in love with me. You were in love, with the idea of me. All that I could be, for you. The potential of me, and what you could mold me into. Well babe, it fucking worked. You molded me into the woman that you had wanted me to be. And within this process, I lost the person that I used to be.

You weren't in love with me. You were in love, with the idea of me. You were in love, with what I could be for you. And not with who I truly was.

~Back in the past, when I was a mirage.

The eyes never lie
They give me away
Every
Single
Time

~ *The gatekeepers of my pain.*

Don't go too far into the woods
Or you'll come out mad
But maybe madness
Is where I want to be
Maybe it isn't so bad?

That's the key with madness
On what scale does it measure?
What if,
You've already reached insanity
And that is your treasure?

Does it matter?
Does it matter?
As long as I am happy
Who really gives a fuck?
Because I want to be free.

~Not caring anymore.

I have been thinking of my old lover
Left somewhere between
Heartache and cold

My uncle once told me,
You brought the winter back with you
All I had wanted
Was someone to hold

Maybe it was fated like this
Some decisions made
Were better than others

And some wins I celebrate
While I still think
Of my ex-lovers

Maybe this is my fate
To be left alone
To prevent the future lovers
From making me their home

~Ice Queen

I have come to realize
That my persona
Would forever be loneliness
I embrace it now
For my heart
Has gotten used to it
One cannot simply understand
The things I have gone through
Or the things I know now
I embrace the loneliness
For it is another friend of mine
One that was never really invited
But always wants to stay

Loneliness is a slow
Grueling pain
Like a poison
Slowly killing you

But the loneliness
Is a reminder
Of a disease
That will never go away

It serves its stupid purpose
As this constant reminder
Of your fucking pain.

~ *The Musings of Depression.*

My soul hurts and my heart aches
My head is tired and my eyes are weary
I am feeling pain
All over my body
Wondering, just wondering
If I will ever
Feel normal again
I held resentment for the world
For not noticing
The pain in my eyes
The constant scream
I was sending
Within my eerie silence
No one cared
To really glance up
To really see
I guess that is what happens
When you are in pain
You are too much of a burden
To have to explain
And that is when I realized
Why people tend to choose

To fight their battles alone
Because there is nothing
That can quite ever
Make them feel at home

Oh Death likes to taunt me
Likes to feast on my soul
To remind me what it's like
To never feel whole

Like a stab to your heart
A reminder of your pain
Where others have gone
You still remain

Maybe other stories are hopeful
Maybe even beautiful at times
But for me it's just torture
Inside my fucking mind

~Make it stop.

God knows I tried
But I am so fucking tired
Of trying

I just
Do not
Want to feel
This much pain
Anymore.

~Please end this.

I'd be lying if I said
I haven't had days
   Where I didn't want to live

   ~ The truth.

When people who have not had Depression
Decide to ask me
What Depression is like
It's not just sadness
No
It's always some kind of fight
The fight against your mind

Depression
Is that voice in your head
That likes to tell you
That you are lonely
That you are nothing
That no one cares for you

It's that voice
That sounds
So much like your own
But it's a disguise
It manipulates you
Day in and day out
But it is not your voice

And when that dark fucker of a voice
Likes to come back
Uninvited
And has the audacity
To tell you things
That aren't true
Tell that voice
To fuck the hell off

~My battles with Depression.

I used to always use my dreams as an escape, to forget the ugliness of reality. But how can I do that now? When I always see you there, taunting me, never allowing me to forget you. You are the cause of my fucking nightmares, the reason why I lose sleep. You have no fucking right, to enter my alternate universe for there is no place for you to stay.

~Breaking and entering different realities.

When your one escape
Becomes haunted
By that one person
You never want to
See again
Darling
That is my version
Of Hell

~Torture

How many times
Will my demons come back?
I am tired of dealing
With these sleepless nights

The ones that plague you
With sadness and fear
And those dark under eye circles
You try so hard to conceal

You drink the black coffee
But it no longer keeps you up
You have become nocturnal
Like a bat alive in the night

I just want my brain to shut off
For it gets exhausting
To fight your own thoughts
A battle that has become
Way too rough

Am I going insane?
Or has insanity found me?
Maybe just maybe
This is how I am meant to be

Like a broken kaleidoscope lens
A distorted way to deal
Is it the beginning?
Or is it the end?

There were things he wanted to see
Places he wanted to go
But when does the dreamer stop dreaming?
When has he succumbed so low?
Does the dreamer give up?
Because there is no reason to fight?
Or does he search for more?
Fighting oblivion of the night?
Are the dreamers stupid?
Have they gone mad?
Why is this world so cold?
It makes me quite sad
What has this world become?
Where insanity is normal
And dreaming is insane?
Was he born in the wrong time?
Was he just being vain?
The dreamer felt lost
Within the sea of souls
The dreamer wanted to find a place
A place he called home
But where does he go?

It gets so confusing
He wants more to know
His body starts to hurt
Because he then starts to wonder
What is he here to learn?
Before his soul sinks under?

I don't know if all of the pain was worth it

But hey,

I wrote fucking poetry.

ILLUSIONS
OF THE SUN

I guess our universes were meant to collide at a certain moment in time. I wonder how different my life would have been if they never did. But when our universes came together, it really felt like fate. I never believed in fate, until I met you. But I was naïve. I had no idea what fate was supposed to feel like. I thought I found my soulmate and that our stars had aligned. But our universes moved at different speeds. Yours faster than mine. I thought we were soulmates, but I could not even fathom, how wrong I truly was. And while I was trying to keep up with your pace, your desires, your needs, my universe was starting to lose control. It slowly started dying, so that yours could burn brighter. It was only later when I realized that this had been your plan all along. To kill my beautiful universe, because it was a threat to yours. And while you were continuing with your act, you made me look like a hopeless fool. A fool, who thought was rising up with you. But darling, we both know how this story unraveled. I got lost in your black hole of darkness. And when my universe exploded, you just threw me out. Like I was trash you no longer wanted. I, had nothing left of me. Nothing to fix myself with.

I didn't know how to start. Where do I even begin? I guess I had to be a star. Do you know how stars are born? Through particles of dust. Broken pieces of the universe. And that's what I was. Broken, lost pieces of matter that no one wanted. Floating, somewhere in oblivion. And maybe this is where I wanted to stay. In nothingness. So I stayed there, in what felt like some infinite eternity. But as I was floating in mere existence, I started to realize that life was passing me by. I was gambling with my time. So slowly, within the infinite darkness that I made my home out of, I created a flicker of light. So small, that it looked like a speck. But what starts as a flicker continues to grow, and it grew and grew. It grew so bright, that I was starting to get my universe back. I started to rebuild it, honor it, and asked my universe for forgiveness. My new universe was now bigger, brighter and stronger than it originally was. And I set my priceless mark on it. Because no one is worth what I can offer. You may have killed my universe darling, but I rebuilt something that you have demolished into something beautiful. And now, even you cannot take that away from me. I don't feel sorry for you. No. I pity you. You could have had so much more. You could have had more than all of the planets and galaxies that resided within my universe. But you chose to liquidate everything I had. No worries love. You are now reading pieces of my universe between these pages. One, you could have been a part of. I am so glad that I built what I did. Thank you. You destroyed parts of me. Parts, I will never get back, or have again. But I seem to have a knack for creating something beautiful, even out of the most petrifying darkness. Thank you. May you read these pages, and hopefully feel something within your closed off conscious. Thank you my love, but fuck you.

~How to rebuild yourself after you have been destroyed.

I wrote you a letter, of all of the things I wish I had said. Or should have said. But instead, listened to the deafening silence of the universe.

I did not have the energy to use my voice, to start standing up for myself. I succumbed to the darkness that started to overcome me. I decided to write down every thought, every feeling, in a careful precision of words.

I coated the papers with the ink of regret and self-pity. Even some tears, managed to fall on the papers, blurring some of the words together. I almost thought about sending an anonymous letter to you, with no return address, so that you couldn't send it back.

In hopes that you would realize, it was me. I am sure you would have known right away, by recognizing my handwriting. Maybe you would call me, or try to make things right. And maybe, just maybe, in an alternate universe, this would have happened. However, my darling, we live in reality. Where tragedies do happen and the world is quite dark.

And when the world is dark, there is only one thing left to do. And that is to start a light. So, I set fire to the letter that you will never receive.

~ The letter that was never sent.

I still feel the burns on my skin. You cannot see them anymore, but the memories of those burns will forever be ingrained in me. I burned so fucking bad, by your petrifying fire. I thought I would die. I think a part of me maybe did. A part of me, that I will never get back. But what was important, was that I rose. I rose the same way as the Phoenix rises from the ashes. And I started my own fire. One, that you will never put out again.

~A powerful forest fire, starts with one tiny spark.

How do you keep yourself from turning into ashes?

When your whole body is on fire, with nothing that is able to extinguish it?

~Rage.

How the fuck
Am I supposed to look inside myself?
And find my soul?
How?
When everything inside of me
Is just trying
So hard not to
Scream.

~On my path of finding my identity.

My freedom was only given within the vicinity of the cage that I was allowed to roam in.

Sometimes I wish
I can turn back time
To when it was better
It was simpler
And we were happier

So that I no longer
Have to deal
With this mess that I have made
Picking up the pieces of us
As a result of this grenade

I am always left wondering
Why I just couldn't
Have made another choice

Because the suffering that occurred
Was not worth it dear one
I should have just
Used my damn voice

~Some decisions will haunt you forever.

How can one person's darkness
Be another person's light?
It is really mind blowing
What human beings
Have the potential
To do
When they have the power
To destroy one
But love another

You feel too much, he said.
This much I knew
But what he didn't understand
Was that I transmuted his pain
Too.

My voice was silenced
For far too long
So do not be surprised
When I fucking
Scream

What I had wanted
Was something real
And something true
But what I received
Was neither
Just lies and facades
That hit me
Blindly in the face
But once the bruises healed
I realized that love
Should not hurt

She loved him
But this love hurt
And she realized
That was not true love

~But that was all she knew.

Why do I always
Fall for broken people?
As I pondered on this thought
Let my mind marinate in this
I finally
Came to a conclusion
And that was
That broken people
Need love too

I freed your words and your reminders
Of what we once were
How happy and hopeful
You must be
With her
We both had wanted
Way too much
Something that
The other person
Could not give
Yes, our story was rough
And as time passed on
I realized something new
One thing was certain
It was never you

~*Letting you go.*

I wonder what you're doing
As you're going through life
Without me
Have you changed at all?
Or did I set you free?
From caring or responsibilities
And commitment and love
Or was that always your plan
One that I wasn't aware of?
You were a master at your game
Feeding me your lies
You got so good
I believed you every time
And now that you are alone
Or maybe with someone new
I hope that I haunt you
For all of the shit
You had put me through
Because you never truly loved me
Or even thought to fucking care
You had crossed a line
One would never dare
You knew if you were honest

You would never stand a chance
You always disappointed me
No matter what it was I had asked
Looks can deceive us
But so can our words
One of the greatest lessons
That life has ever taught me
Was to never lose your self-worth

I actually do wonder
Do soulmates even exist?
I know they do
I see it for others
As they are in bliss
I think they are lucky
Lucky they definitely are
Maybe because they have
What I had always wanted
Maybe love isn't fated for me
Maybe, just maybe
It's because I am haunted

Don't get too close to the sun
For you might get burned
Even the brightest things
Can cause harm

~*Illusions of the sun*

I think the whole problem with love is this:
People fall in love
 With what they want to see
 Instead of
 What is actually there

 ~Mirages

I live through my imagination
So that my perception of the world
Looks a little better
Than what the reality
Actually is.

~*Avoiding Pain.*

What do I want?
I want someone
To not disappoint me
Because of my own
Lack of judgement

I want someone
To tell me
I am prettier
Than all of the stars
That are above

I want someone
To be
What I want them
To be

All of these things
Ironic
Isn't it?

A hopeless romantic
Just wanting
To avoid heartbreak

As an expert in pain
I do not think
That pain
Is the worst feeling
To feel

No

Numbness is

Sometimes it is better
To feel something
Even if it is not always
What you want to feel
Than to not feel anything

At all

Someone once told me
That when you cannot
Fall asleep at night
There must be someone
Somewhere in the world
Thinking of you

So when I cannot
Sleep well through the night
Is it because
You are thinking of me
And all that was right?

~Just a late-night thought.

I think about it all. The adventures that we had. The walks that we went on. The laughs that made our stomachs hurt. I cannot help but remember it sometimes. It was real, what we had. But only, when you remember the good parts of the story.

And when I am deep in our memories, where it almost feels real again, I cannot help but feel that pang in my stomach. Some moments I remember more vividly than others. The special ones are still kept, deep in my heart.

I think about it all. Where we went wrong, but also what we did right. I know it is stupid, for me to think of you and what we used to have. And sometimes I wonder, if you think about me too? Do you remember me? Do you miss the things, that were only ours to share?

But before I get too lost within these thoughts, I quickly gather myself. I start to realize, that it is so pointless to think about it all. Because I am almost certain, that I am never on your mind.

You have forgotten me. And some may ask, *How am I certain of this? How do I know this to be true?* Well darling, I was not your first love, nor will I be your last.

I wish the stars had lined up in our universes. I wanted to look at them, admire them, and love them unconditionally. The stars would have shown us a beautiful picture of our future, where it would have been the two of us. But like any sad story, our stars didn't line up. It was the universe telling us that we weren't meant to be. Some universes collide, while others fall apart. I still think of you, as I look up to the night sky. I can't help but wonder if you do too. But I guess it doesn't matter now anyways.

~These thoughts are a waste of my time.

Don't be disappointed
When her universe
Is nothing
Compared to mine

I was a comet
You were lucky enough to see me
As I don't always pass by
In everyone's
Lifetime

~When you let go of fate.

The winter had passed
But the coldness
In her heart
Still remains

~Heartbreak can do so much damage.

She guards her heart
With coldness
But with strength
And she hopes that one day
She can give her heart
To someone
Who can take care of it
This time

~ The pang of being single.

I hope that the next time we meet
Because it will happen
My presence will startle you
And I hope you regret
All of the wrong
That you had done to me
You will realize
The woman that you had
And the woman that you lost

~It was your loss darling, not mine.

Why are the rebels
The people that are bad for you
Are the same people
That make you feel the most alive?

~Adrenaline can be so addicting.

Damned are the beautiful minds
That overthink and stay up all night
Going through the scenarios
Of what cannot be
Like some lovers
One, who is lost at sea

But this is not a happy ending
There is no more hope
The other half, who is lost
Is not coming home

This is pure heartbreak
A love forever lost
This story shows
That love is not so easy
As one may have thought

We used to float while we danced
We used to look up at the stars
We used to laugh like we were drunk
But maybe, just maybe
We were drunk
Drunk in love
We used to get tangled in each other
By the warmth of our bed
We used to listen to songs
That got stuck in our heads
We used to fantasize
A future together
As we really believed
That we had found forever

~*What used to be.*

She loves coffee in the morning
And whiskey at night
   Some days are really hard
   Some days she doesn't want to fight

   But she fights with herself
   Her mind is a dark place
   Some days she wishes
   There was a way to escape

   Why does the world
   Have to be cruel at times?
   Isn't there enough pain?
   Aren't there enough lies?

   What is the purpose?
   When she seems to find darkness
   She has a fascination with black holes
   Letting herself be taunted

Maybe she will realize
That the stars are beautiful too
And hopefully they will remind her
That she can live anew

~Searching for answers

Once you get off the high
Of being called pretty
You get back to the low
Of believing that you're ugly

~Society's cruel games

Why is it so easy?
To see beauty
In everything else
But not yourself?

Perfection, is a deadly poison to drink, my dear.

It does not take much
To break a person to pieces
With words that they will never forget
Although the time will pass
The words
Will always remain

~Choose your words wisely.

I keep writing and writing
Am I emptying my mind
   Of my insanity?
   Or am I feeding it
   More and more?

~*The musings of a poet.*

I am a matryoshka
How many layers
Of my façade
Will you have to
Pull out
To get to
My core?

~ *The layers of me.*

Do you hear me?
Can you see me visiting?
Sometimes it is a curse
To be the one left living

~Grief

You wonder why you're here
When others have gone
   You start to ponder on life
   And remember you're not God

   Oh life can be funny
   More like cruel at times
   Nothing makes sense
   And you then start to cry

   It's true what they say
   That the good ones die young
   But you don't know how much
   Your departure had stung

   Oh please give me a sign
   Something I can understand
   But I realize that life
   I cannot always comprehend

   I know you're somewhere out there
   Maybe close or far away
   But then I realize in my heart
   You were never meant to stay

I close the curtains and lock the doors
I do not want anyone to see me
Or hear me
My soul begins to wail
As I hold back my tears
But pretty soon
The flood cannot be held back
And it rushes out like a river
One, that cannot be contained
My soul starts to release
All of the things
That I have been hurt by
The unfairness of the world
The scenes of obscurity
And the injustice
The way of life
That is unfeasible to live
I try to be quiet
Because it was ingrained in me
To not show the world
When you are weak and vulnerable
In the face of a crisis
But darling

The feelings that you feel
Are what cause you to heal
And may you not be afraid
Of the darkest parts of your soul
Because in doing so
You will be flowing with the river
That rushes through
Instead of treading against it

~Feelings, are meant to be felt.

God, you love the swings, he said.
Oh yes, the swings love me, I replied.
But you look like a child, he said.

But…
I am a child you see
A child
In a grown-up body
This child never had
Enough love
So when that child
Grew up
She went on
Searching
For this so-called *Love*
And she went looking for it
In places
And men
But all that she found
Was none of the above
She wanted an escape
To numb out her pain
The world was a dark place

A step closer to oblivion
Seemed like a fun game
How far could she go?
Within the darkness
That resided in her soul
Will the darkness consume her?
And make her feel whole?
She started to realize
How far she had gone
How far in the black hole
She really went on
Was there a way
For her to get out?
Does she stay in hell?
Does she find a way out?
She had learned her lesson
Which made her realize
That she needed light
May that light burn the darkness
Destroy the shame that she carried
May that light shine ahead
And let that light remind her
That she had made it

Through her dark night
She had made it
She survived

~Trauma

How beautiful is it?
To look back at previous moments
That you thought were the worst
Because you were going through
Your reoccurring nightmare
At that point in time
But now you are here
In the present moment
Truly alive.

~In hindsight

I am so fucking proud of myself
For living through every single moment
Where I had wanted to die

~Stay

THE BALANCE
OF EXISTENCE

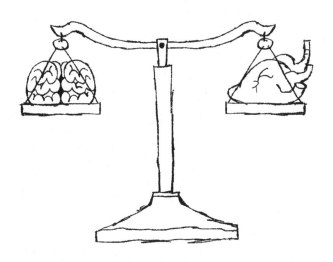

The first joy you feel
After Depression ravaged your soul
Is one of the most exhilarating feelings
To have the privilege to feel
After being in darkness for so long

~It was a shock to my system.

I remember being invalidated
For feeling depressed and even mad
Like I had no right to fucking feel
And had to be grateful
For what I had

But what happens when you don't
Find gratitude in your life?
Does that make you a terrible person?
Does that make you alright?

What happens when your brain
Has been poisoned throughout the years?
Being told you are nothing
As it feasted on your fears

How do you re-program your brain
When it was on survival mode for so long?
The world doesn't give you instructions
On how to be strong

How do you pick yourself up?
When you don't even trust yourself?
What I learned through my pain
Was that it was best left
On the shelf

Push the pain away
Don't let it haunt your soul
No one wanted pain
People carried enough
Of their own

Your feelings are valid
Even if no one believes them
Because it is society
That is broken
Beyond any mend

So fuck society
And all of their wicked games
You are absolutely worthy
So let go of your shame

And if no one sees your victories
Just know that I see you
Because I know what it is like
To not feel like someone
Who is worth more than a few

~*You will make it.*

Darling
I deserved better
And still do

Be kind to your heart. It will take on some battles.

Maybe
Just maybe
    You were trying to make
    The puzzle piece
    That was him
    Fit inside
    Your own puzzle
    But what if he wasn't
    The right puzzle piece
    For your heart?

Don't be sad love
He doesn't deserve your love
But you do
He may have already moved on
But you should too

~You deserve to move on from the pain.

The sun never fails to fascinate me
Most people love it
Because it brings warmth and light
But you have to be careful
Because many do not realize
How badly you can get burned
When you are out under it
For too long

~Relationships are like that too.

I used to be a wilted flower
One that would not bloom
I had died
How could I begin again?
How could I be a flower
When it would not bloom
The first time around?
I had to wait through
The coldest winter yet
And with the new spring
Slowly
New flowers started to appear
I began to admire their beauty
And slowly learned
To admire mine
I learned to grow
In the harshest conditions
Instead of dying
It was only then
When my own flowers
Started to be the most beautiful
Of all the gardens
But people admired them

For what they looked like
Not for what they overcame
They were admired for the wrong reasons
But I learned to appreciate my flowers
For all that they were
And did the same for myself
You will see my flowers one day
Everywhere you walk
They will remind you of me
Of what we were
And what we had
The potential to be
But I will only be
A distant memory
And my flowers
Won't be picked by you
Since you will try so hard
To forget me

I want the white tulips to grow
To show that I still am
Forgiven and loved
It is the beauty in nature
That is way too good for us
I look to the field
But I don't see them yet
I come back every day and I pray
That these white tulips will see me
And say it's okay
It's okay to let go
And that it is necessary
And not even an option
To love yourself
Again

~*Forgiveness*

I gave myself permission
To write about everything
And anything
That decided
To cross my brilliant mind
I let myself write
No matter what others
Wanted to find
I gave myself permission
To write about my pain
And my sadness
How did I
Survive for so long?
With my little dose
Of madness?
I like being different
Quirky, strange and odd
They are all parts of me
That were never ever
Flawed

So how do you fix yourself?
When the world has left you broken?
What do you do?
When your heart has finally spoken?

My heart was shattered in pieces
From the people that have dropped it
I didn't know how to fix it
I was thinking I had lost it

You have to sit with your pain
And honor your past
You will then realize
That this too shall pass

It will all be okay
There is no light without darkness
We are beings of polarity
We won't always feel haunted

We are on our own journey
One with many twists and turns
We won't always understand
This long winding road

But I want you to remember
That when life gets hard
Remember the end of the road
When you come back to God

I let the melancholy own me
Let it feast on my soul
Wondered why I was here
As I felt no control

I spent so much time
Feeling sad for existing
But my will kept on going
Even though I was resisting

Resisting my evolution
I was scared of this change
I felt I wasn't worthy
It always felt so strange

The thing about healing is
It's not a linear graph
It is anything but
Although you may laugh

Healing takes time
It's an up and down journey
There will be days where you plead
And ask God for mercy

It's a battle against yourself
You may not always feel strong
But I can tell you this
It will be **you** all along

It will be **you**
Who will get through
The nights you truly thought
That you were getting better
But end up slipping up
Once again

It will be **you**
Who will pull yourself
Out of fucking hell
Even though you liked burning
Again and again

It will be **you**
Who will finally win
As you deserve to
Right in the end

~The power is in your hands.

She is a bird
That will now use
    Her newly found freedom
    To fly
    Wherever the fuck
    She pleases
    If you make her feel trapped
    She will fly away
    And never return

~ The essence of her freedom.

The people that come back
When they are bored
Or when it is best
Convenient for them
Are not your friends
They are people
That are there
To waste your time
And take your energy
And when they no longer
Need you anymore
They disappear forever
And never return
But your time darling
Is something
That you will never get back

~Use your time wisely.

I used to think that friends are permanent
But it is okay if they are not
Some friends will help you grow
However, sometimes
They may instead
Hold you back
And honey
It is okay
To let them go
For the friends that are no longer there
To support you
To love you
To care
Friends that make you feel
Like you're gasping for air
Are no longer your *friends*
It is time
To let them all go

~Don't look back.

I used to hate you
Because you were the one
That shattered me
I gave up
I drowned
I felt death
Even flowers have breakthroughs
When they rise in the spring
And I too
Had my breakthrough
I reflected
I rose
I started to fight back
I lost my armor
I lost myself
But my will was strong
And I continued
To move on
And without you
I wouldn't have realized
The person that I
Truly am
So thank you

You shattered me
But now
I am going to be
The stars within all of the galaxies

~*Taking my power back.*

She would rather die
Than feel this much pain
But pain
Is our greatest teacher
And necessary for growth
So growing pains
Hurt

Do not ever belittle someone's pain
Because it is something
You do not understand

~May everyone know this.

Poetry is an expression
Of the deepest parts of my soul
It allows me to use my voice
Which makes me feel whole

Poetry makes me feel safe
To tell the stories my heart knows
But my eyes tell you the truth
Of how much I have grown

Poetry saved my life
When I didn't want to live
It pushed me to keep going
To have something to give

Poetry challenged me
To heal myself
To sit with the darkest
Parts of my Hell

Poetry is subjective
Not everyone will like your words
But I realized
That is not the fucking point
I just wanted to be heard

~Poetry is an art, a masterpiece not everyone will understand.

The head and the heart
Are always at war
When one screams *try again*
The other says *no more*

~ *The constant battle, between what you say and how you feel.*

You can't blame them
Completely
They loved you in the way
They knew how to love
But that doesn't mean
That their love
Was enough
For you

~Please realize this.

Some people
Stay up late
To talk to the moon
And ask questions
About their fate

While I think
That the moon is fantastic
I look for something else
In that vast sky

I look for the promises you told me
And how they ended up being lies
I look for your reflection
And the way that you smiled

I look to the sky
For something that was once mine
I look for some answers
That I can't seem to find

But as I look to the sky
At the diamonds within the darkness
I realized that
There were many things
I had wanted

But to be human
Is to accept
That not everything
Can go precisely
As you had planned

~Lessons I learned from the night sky.

People have no problem
Breaking you into pieces
Because they are not the ones
Cleaning up the mess

~But you have yourself.

I think pain is inevitable
There is no escaping it
But I also think
That it is what you learn from the pain
Is what truly matters

You can take your pain
And turn it into something beautiful
Yes.
But do not for one moment
Underestimate
The strength you had
And still have
That you relied on
To survive that pain.

~You are so powerful.

In the midst of healing
Do not forget
That you are human
And that you are also meant
To just live

~ The balance of existence.

I think it was humorous
To see people
Surprised by my happiness
As if sadness and self-pity
Was my permanent persona
One that would never leave
But then I started to think
How long did I bask within my sadness?
Maybe it was a good thing to see their shock
Because maybe that meant
I was finally
Moving on

It is such a beautiful thing
To start falling in love
With your life
Again

I now realize
That things will never be the same
As they were in 2019
Before everything happened

But maybe now
I don't want things
To be the same
As they were before

And I think that's
What fucking growth is

NEW

BEGINNINGS

I bless the Earth
And I bless the sky
For the fact that your soul
Was able to find mine

7 billion people
Well technically almost eight
And it feels like we were merged
By the work of fate

For you have taken the time
To see the hurt in my eyes
You have been able
To look past my disguise

You like me for my authenticity
My flaws and my struggles too
It takes a special type of person
To see this all through

I hope that this is everything
That you want it to be
Too

For you I'll take a gamble
Even though I'll lose it all
May it all be worth it
It's the jump before the fall

I think it will be enough
To calm my restless heart
Inside I am a rebel
An extravagant work of art

I will listen to my heart
The first time I ever did
For my brain was my top priority
Logic always seemed to win

I may have to deal
With the consequences of my decision
But it is something I am bypassing
Trying to act with more precision

Who the fuck knows?
It might be a forever high
A fun little ride
A rollercoaster of a lifetime

We were two little owls
Saw beauty in the night
Found treasure in the darkness
Others could not find

We created our own world
Where others have drowned
Somedays we were floating
Our feet barely on the ground

There were some days
We cried the river of tears
Some days we smiled
As we battled our fears

The journey was harsh
As we wore our scars
Proof of the battles
Within our poor hearts

Letting go truly
Has been the hardest thing for me
But that was until
You walked into my life
That's when I finally felt free

I was looking for happiness
In whatever I could find
    But it was later that I realized
    That was not true happiness

    I realized that true happiness
    Is the wholeness of your soul
    Being completely content
    That is the goal

    But there was something about you
    When you came around
    I didn't need you to complete me
    It was something profound

    You just added to the cup of my happiness
    Made me feel fully free
    And that is when I realized
    This is how it should be

    ~You awakened my soul.

In a galaxy full of stars
Where we shined so bright
The infinite was ours
We were ready to take flight

We loved the feeling of falling
We weren't scared of the ground
We trusted our love
To stay safe and sound

The universe was wide
Our love stretched very far
We were giddy with excitement
We were reaching for the stars

Our love was a comet
A rare lifetime event
You would not be able to explain it
To anyone you have ever met

I write stories with my mind
Into little clues
For others to find
And maybe one day
They will realize
That my so-called *insanity*
Was in fact
My *creativity*

What I love about Poetry
Is that you will always understand
A certain piece
So much so
When you desperately
Need to
And that's why Poetry is
Magical
Because when you find it
Or technically
When the words find you
They find you
At the right time
When you need them
To.

I dreamed of a city
That I wanted to see
With my very own eyes
I saw it in my sleep

Once I see this special place
Where desire has never left me
It will nourish my soul
And I will finally reach
A new epiphany

~Dreaming

I drove back to Chicago
To breathe in that cold air
Something about that city
Always brings me back there

This city has a pulse
If you listen to its heart
People love New York City and LA
But Chicago has my heart

It has my upbringing
My happy memories, my beginning
My love for Lake Michigan
The nostalgia leaves me grinning

I wish more people
Saw the beauty that I see
And what I feel
Within this city

~I love you Chicago.

How beautiful are the snowflakes?
As they fall to the ground
They keep falling and falling
Without making a sound

And soon without notice
There is a blanket of white
The days start to get shorter
To see more of the night

Not many appreciate winter
Because of its cold
But the beauty of winter
Is that you shed all the old

Embrace this new darkness
When you can't have the light
Darkness isn't all that bad
It will all be alright

You always open my mind to new things
Challenge me to think outside the box
Have me question what I already thought
It keeps me on my toes
In a good way
I really do like
Having a friend like you
Someone I can joke with and have fun
With ease and no complications
I wish more people
Were extravagant and simple
As you

~*Appreciation*

Some people like to talk to the moon
I like talking to the stars

~*The Galaxy, is so fucking beautiful.*

The more miracles you believe in
The more magic you will see

~And vice versa.

I like my solitude
It makes me feel better
Than being around people
That make me feel alone

~Inner peace

Don't listen to the lies
That our ill society
Tries to tell you to be

Instead

Listen to the words
That your soul
Needs you to be

~Follow your inner compass.

Forgive yourself
For all of the mistakes
That you have made

The past cannot be changed
And the future has not been written
But the present is still here

So please take advantage
Of every moment
That you have

Because one day
You will see
Just how quickly
Life passes you by

~Just live.

You make mistakes
Because you are human
This is the process
Of learning and growing
Please do not ever
Forget that

~It's all for your evolution.

Being an Empath
Is not a sign of weakness
But a sign of great strength
What beauty you have
To be able to see the world
Through the lens of compassion

Age can have so many meanings, but also none.

~Our souls cannot be measured by numbers.

No longer am I scared of winter
I fully embrace the cold
This coldness is cleansing
It is healing for my soul

Winter is water
May this season wash away
All that served its purpose
And what no longer needs to stay

We ride the waves of life
In oscillations
That go up and down

When we are riding
The wave of despair
We think we will drown

But slowly with persistence
You will then come to find
That the wave you were worried about
Ended up being so aligned

~We are the boats of surrender.

Your body
Does so much for you
Your body protects you
Even though you don't think so
It does
Your body loves you
It regenerates you
Every
Single
Day
It's about time now
That you finally return the favor
And give your body
The love it deserves
That it always had
And still has
For you

~Self-Love

It gets better
What once was bad
Becomes good
What once was broken
Becomes mended
What once was dark
Turns into light
It gets better
You just have to make it through
The harsh times
In order to see it
For yourself

~Healing

I am light
I am love
I was sent
From the heavens above

We are all beautiful
Down to the core
And you need to remember
That you are worth
So much more.

I look into the mirror
Proud of myself
For how far
I have come

Realizing too
That I should have never
Been ashamed
For my mere existence

~You matter. You matter more than you even realize.

I saw the Bald Eagle fly
Right over my head
I felt a sense of comfort
For my journey ahead

For the longest time
I felt so much doubt
And so much uncertainty
I didn't know at all
What my life was about

But as soon as I surrendered
And started trusting my path
The universe blessed me
And showed me the power
That I always had

~Thank you

In a field full of flowers
She was the one
  Floating in the yellow
  When the day was finally done

  The sun came down
  As a way to remind her
  The journey up ahead
  Had no one else beside her

  She knew she was strong
  So she looked into nature
  Because she knew the next step
  Would be something major

  ~Mother Earth was there for her.

I want to thank everyone
That took a part in my healing
Bless you
Especially to the ones
That stayed
When I was completely unbearable
And to the ones that listened
To the same depressing stories
That I would tell
About my sadness
And feeling like hell
I want to thank everyone
That sat with my broken pieces
And helped me put some of them
Back together again
I want to thank the healers
That took out the dark matter
That resided in my soul
Thank you for showing me
The way back
To myself

Right on
My destined path

~*Endless Gratitude*

And the old parts
That no longer serve her
Will die and die
And from the ashes
A new reborn soul
Will rise and rise
And she will continue
To rise
Again and again

~New Beginnings.

Acknowledgements

For the sake of privacy, I will only mention the first names of the people that I want to thank and recognize. I would like to first send my deepest gratitude to my parents, who have always supported my writing process and encouraged me even more to write this book. Thank you. Your support means everything to me. I would like to thank my dear friend Geovic, who kept pushing me to keep the darker pieces of my poetry, saying, "Great Literature was never a walk in the park". Thank you. You were right. I would like to thank my dear friend Laura, who always reminded me to take care of myself, when I was so immersed in getting this book completed. Thank you. I definitely needed to take those breaks. I want to thank my friend Eve. I appreciated all of your support that you have given me throughout this entire writing process. Thank you. I want to thank Shannon, who came into my life quite recently, but has already made a huge impact on my spirit. You have helped me overcome so much. Thank you for encouraging me to get my words out, to use my voice, and for pushing me to continue even though I was doubting myself. I know there are many more people who I have forgotten to thank, but I feel their overwhelming support with me. I am grateful for the community that is following me and reminds me of my strength. I also want to thank all of the readers, who have picked up this book, and have read it until the very end. I am so grateful for all of you. Writing has been such a therapeutic process for me, especially in the times of my greatest challenges. I hope you too, were able to get something out of this. I wish everyone healing and happiness, since that is what we all truly deserve.

Made in the USA
Monee, IL
21 May 2021